HP

If

Richmond upon Thames Libraries

Renew online at www.richmond.gov.uk/libraries

LONDON BOROUGH OF
RICHMOND UPON THAMES

D1493107

90710 000 492 386

Books by Steven Lenton

GENIE AND TEENY: MAKE A WISH

GENIE AND TEENY: WISHFUL THINKING

Coming soon

GENIE AND TEENY: THE WISHING WELL

GENIE AND TEENY

WISHFUL THINKING

Steven Lenton

HarperCollins *Children's Books*

First published in Great Britain by
HarperCollins *Children's Books* in 2021
HarperCollins *Children's Books* is a division of HarperCollins*Publishers* Ltd
HarperCollins*Publishers*
1 London Bridge Street
London SE1 9GF

www.harpercollins.co.uk

HarperCollins*Publishers*
1st Floor, Watermarque Building, Ringsend Road
Dublin 4, Ireland

1

ISBN 978–0–00–840823-7

Steven Lenton asserts the moral right to be identified as the author
and illustrator of the work.

A CIP catalogue record for this title is available from the British Library.

Printed and bound using 100% renewable electricity at CPI Group (UK) Ltd

FOR VANESSA, JULIE, NAOMI AND CARMEN:
THE BRILLIANT TEAM AT BOOK NOOK, HOVE. SL X

HELLO, READER!

The last time we saw Genie and Teeny, they were fast asleep inside Grant's teapot – sorry, I mean his MAGIC LAMP. (Grant is rather insistent that it is absolutely, definitely **NOT** a teapot, if you remember, so let's go with that.) And this is exactly where we find them this morning. Slightly dribbly, rather windy ***PARP*** and **VERY** asleep.

Shall we try to wake them up?

Give them a shake

OR

maybe turn them upside down . . . ?

No joy. We'll have to shout them awake . . .

After three, ready?

One,

two,

THREE –

WAKE UP, GRANT AND TEENY!

Gosh, even THAT didn't work – they must be **REALLY** tired.

But wait! Who's this? Oh, it's Teeny's owner, Tilly!

CHAPTER 1

WHERE ARE YOU, TEENY?

'TEENY! TEENY, WHERE ARE YOU?' Tilly called.

Tilly couldn't think where Teeny could be. He usually slept on her bed, so she was worried when he wasn't there. She had looked everywhere for him upstairs, so now she was searching downstairs.

She looked in the cupboards, the drawers, around the living room, even in the toilet! But Teeny was nowhere to be seen.

Tilly started to cry. She had only just found Teeny after Grant had rescued him from the scary Lavinia Lavender and already she had lost him again! Then she heard an odd noise.

PFFFFFFFT

What was that?

TRUMP

'WHO'S THERE?'

It sounded like it was coming from the teapot but it couldn't be. She picked it up and looked down the spout but it was too dark to see anything. So she lifted the lid and gasped.

The gasp woke Grant and Teeny up. There, right in front of them, was a **GIANT EYEBALL** staring at them.

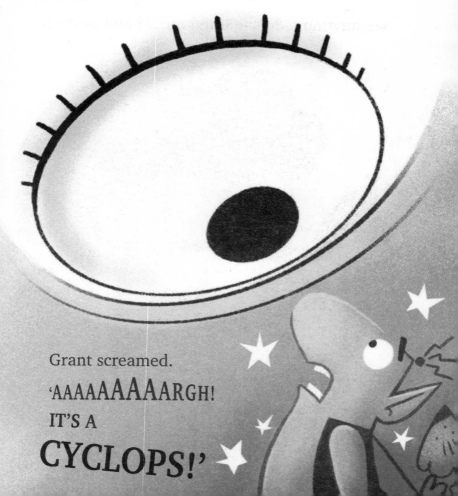

Grant screamed.

'AAAAAAAAAARGH!
IT'S A
CYCLOPS!'

In spite of not knowing what a cyclops was, Teeny felt sure that it wasn't a cyclops at all and that it was really just his owner, Tilly. He leapt towards her, landing on her nose.

'Teeny, you're . . . TINY! And who . . . who is this?' she asked, bewildered.

Grant appeared in a cloud of sparkly turquoise smoke *POOOF* and hovered in front of Tilly.

'I think you'd better sit down, Tilly, and I'll make you a nice cup of tea.' Grant snapped his fingers and a cup and saucer appeared in Tilly's hands.

'Er, there's no tea in here, just a pea?' Tilly said, puzzled.

'I am Grant the genie and, as you have just witnessed, I'm not great at magic or making wishes – which is how I got banished from Genie World by the genie queen, landed here on Earth, found this new lamp—'

'Er, it's a teapot—' started Tilly.

'DON'T INTERRUPT ME, PLEASE,' said Grant. 'I found this new LAMP, met Teeny and helped him get back home. Lots of other funny and scary stuff happened in between, but you'd have to read Book One if you want to know everything.' Grant winked at Teeny.

'I don't believe it! A **REAL** genie? **WOW!'** said Tilly. 'Thank you so much for helping Teeny to find us. It sounds like quite an adventure! But you must be missing Genie World – can we help you to get home?'

'TILLY! WHO ARE YOU TALKING TO DOWN THERE?' Tilly's mum called from upstairs.

'ER, NOBODY, MUM. I'm listening to the radio.'

Tilly clicked the radio on and looked at the time. 'Yikes! I'm going to be late for school! But I can't leave you both here!'

Then Tilly noticed a letter from school on the side. It read:

BRING YOUR PET TO SCHOOL!

FRIDAY 9 JULY

MAKE SURE TO BRING FOOD,
WATER AND POO BAGS
IF REQUIRED.

THERE WILL BE A PET PARADE AT
12 P.M.

**PRIZE FOR MOST
TALENTED PET.**

'That's today! **FANTASTIC!** Grant, please could you turn Teeny back to normal size so I can take him to school with me?'

Grant smiled and clicked his fingers.

'ABSOLUTELY!'

Teeny grew.
And grew.
AND GREW
until he was filling the entire kitchen, his paws and tail sticking out of the windows and door.

'NOTHING, MUM! I'm just packing my rucksack!' Tilly hastily called back. 'Erm, he's a bit TOO big, Grant!' a rather squashed Tilly whispered.

'WHOOPS, sorry!' Grant replied, shaking out his hands and moving his head from side to side, as if he were preparing to do some exercise. Then he clicked his fingers a second time and – **WHOOOOSH!** – Teeny was back to his regular size.

He licked Tilly's face and she giggled, gave him a **BIG** squeeze and then attached his lead to his collar. 'Grant, you can tell me more about Genie World on the way to school,' said Tilly. 'If you stay small, you can sit on my shoulder. We'd better not let anyone else see you yet, though. Is that okay?'

'ABSOLUTELY. I'll be as good as gold, as quiet as a mouse, as silent as a pancake. You won't even know I'm there,' Grant said, crossing his heart.

Tilly grabbed her lunchbox from the fridge and put it in her rucksack along with Grant's teapot. Then she put on her coat. 'I'M OFF TO SCHOOL, MUM. **SEE YOU LATER!**' she shouted up the stairs.

'DID YOU BRUSH YOUR TEETH . . . ?' Mum shouted back. But it was too late for dental reminders. Tilly, Grant and Teeny were out of the door!

CHAPTER 2

ON THE WAY TO SCHOOL

Tilly hurried along the pavement with Teeny at her side and Grant perched on her shoulder like a turquoise parrot.

Grant was super excited at seeing lots of new things on their way to school and couldn't help but shout things out as they

went along:

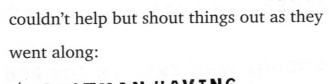

'A POSTMAN HAVING
A WEE BEHIND A BUSH!'

'A LADY HANGING SOME BIG KNICKERS ON A WASHING LINE!'

'SOMEONE WHO TROD IN DOG POO IS PRETENDING THEY HAVEN'T!'

(We've all been there.)

'Shhhhhh, Grant, be quiet! You'll get us into trouble.'

'Sorry, Tilly. I just get so excited at seeing all these things in real life!'

Grant was ticking off all the things in his book – THE GUIDE TO EARTHLY EARTHLINGS – as they strolled along the pavement.

'So, Grant, why can't you just magic yourself back to Genie World?' Tilly asked.

'Well, in genie law, if you're banned from Genie World, you can't go back until you do something SPECTACULARLY AMAZINGLY WONDERFUL for the genie queen, and because I accidentally turned her into a snake I think I'll have to do something truly EXTRAORDINARY before I'm allowed back home.'

'That sounds awfully mean. I'm sure there'll be a way we can help you,' Tilly reassured him.

'OH NO!' Tilly interrupted herself.

'What's the matter?'

'Don't look now, but see that boy over there on his scooter? That's Billy Krump, the school bully. Don't make eye contact with him when we walk past and please don't shout anything out!'

'ABSOLUTELY. I'll be as quiet as a cucumber!' said Grant.

Tilly looked into the sky and whistled as

they walked past Billy.

'LOOK, IT'S THE SCHOOL BULLY, BILLY KRUMP—

OOOPS!'

Grant put his hand over his mouth, looked

apologetically at Tilly and flew back into his
teapot, embarrassed.

'OI, TILLY TELLTALE, what did you just
call me?' Billy shouted angrily.

'Er, it wasn't me, Billy. I'm just walking
to school with my dog Teeny. All perfectly
normal, nothing to see here. Must dash! Bye!'

'You're not allowed dogs in school, you
WALLY,' he mocked.

'You are when it's Bring Your Pet to
School Day, Billy,' Tilly retorted.

Billy looked a bit sad. 'Oh, I, er, didn't
realise.'

'What pet are you bringing, Billy?' Tilly
asked.

'I don't have a pet. Dad won't let me. Er, I mean, pets are stupid. I mean, look at your **STUPID MUTT** – looks like a bog brush with a collar on! And what kind of silly name is "Teeny"? A stupid one, that's what,' Billy heckled.

Teeny growled at Billy.

'And what's that in your bag?'

'Nothing.'

'Looks like a yellow teapot!'

'It's a LAMP!' huffed Grant.

'Oh, THIS!' replied Tilly quickly to cover up Grant's voice. 'It's, er, Teeny's teapot. I'm going to . . . draw it in art class today.'

'Why's it sparkling – and is that a pair of eyes peeking through the crack in the side?'

'You're just seeing things, Billy, and we're going to be late for school. BYE!'

Tilly turned on her heel and sped on, then she craned her neck round to Grant. 'Phew, that was close! Grant, please be more careful to stay quiet and out of sight!'

'Sorry, Tilly,' said Grant as he sat back on her shoulder, then he turned round and, not being able to help himself, stuck his tongue out at Billy.

Billy blinked in disbelief, jumped on his scooter and followed Tilly to school. What WAS it about that teapot? And what had that weird blue thing been on her shoulder . . . ?

CHAPTER 3
PETS AND PUPILS

Tilly stopped at the school gates. 'You'd better hop back into the teapot, Grant. I'll let you know when the coast is clear.'

'Aye, aye, Tilly!' Grant saluted and he whooshed back into the teapot inside the rucksack.

Tilly took a deep breath, looked around her, then walked into the schoolyard . . .

There before her eyes were **HUNDREDS** of pets of all shapes and sizes with their owners.

There was Ryan Rollins and his rabbit, Ruby.

Sam Smithers and her stick insect, Sticky.

Jayden Jenkins and
his gerbil, Jack.

And Beth Bramage
and her Beetle, Biggles.

To name but a few.

Hmmm, quite boring pets really, thought Tilly. *If only everyone knew I had a genie in my bag!*

When the school bell sounded, the children and their pets marched into the school hall for morning assembly. Tilly kept her rucksack slightly open on her lap so Grant could see what was going on through the crack in the teapot. Billy Krump sat behind them and kept a suspicious eye on Tilly.

The headmaster, Mr Wiggins, walked on to the stage holding a tissue over his nose.

'His hair looks like he's got a ferret on his head!' Grant whispered from the teapot.

Tilly giggled and whispered back,

'His nickname is Wiggy Wiggins because everyone thinks he's wearing a wig.'

'Good morning, boys, girls and – a-a-a-a-A-ACHOoooo! – PETS. As you all know, I am – ah, ah, ah, ah, ah, AH, ACHOOOOOOO!

allergic to all animals, but welcome to our first (and hopefully last) Bring Your Pet to School Day, an important day that will hopefully highlight the importance of learning about, caring for and socialising animals. Now, is there anyone here today who has **NOT** brought a pet to school?'

The hall fell silent except for a squeaky trump from a rather flatulent French bulldog.

'Put up your hand if you have **NOT** brought in a pet.'

Billy Krump slowly raised his hand and everyone turned and stared at him.

Billy looked embarrassed. '**WOT?** I don't want a stupid pet anyway!'

'Billy Krump, you can be my official tissue-box holder for the day. Come to my office straight after assembly. **ACHOOOOOO!**'

Giggles echoed around the school hall as Billy went red and folded his arms in a grump.

'He's in a right Billy Krump grump!' Grant giggled to Tilly.

Suddenly Teeny spotted Carol Carty's cat, Carla, and leapt towards it.

The cat shrieked and ran around the hall, through chair legs and teachers' legs and eventually up a curtain. Teeny chased it, weaving round the legs of several members of staff, and jumped up at the curtain, pulling all the teachers with him. All the other pets in the hall started **BARKING**, squawking, **FLAPPING** and **SNAPPING!**

Tilly chased after him shouting, 'TEENY, STOP!', leaving her rucksack on her seat.

Billy Krump saw his chance and opened Tilly's rucksack and grabbed the teapot, putting one hand over the lid and a thumb over the spout. Then he ran to the boys' toilets . . .

'WHAT'S GOING ON

OVER THERE?'

shouted Mr Wiggins. With a tissue over his nose, he walked over to Teeny, picked him up by the scruff of his neck and handed him back to Tilly.

'I presume this is YOUR dog causing a kerfuffle, Tilly Tickleton?'

'Yes, Mr Wiggins. I'm very sorry, Mr Wiggins.'

'I should think so! Now I don't want to hear

a peep from you or your dog again, EXCEPT at the **Pet Parade** later today! Now, everyone, take your pets QUIETLY to your

-A-A-A-ACHOOOOO!

– first class of the morning.'

'YES, MR WIGGINS,' chanted the children as they all turned and started walking out of the hall and down the corridor.

Tilly picked up her rucksack. It suddenly felt very light. She opened it and instantly felt sick. The teapot had

GONE!

CHAPTER 4

A SNAPPY DECISION

In the boys' loos Billy locked the door behind him, sat on one of the toilets and looked at the teapot. He shook it from side to side. He rattled it. He turned it upside down. And then he just looked puzzled.

Inside the teapot Grant was wondering what was going on. All his hats, cushions and potion bottles toppled down around him.

'Is everything okay out there, Tilly?' he called. 'Is the coast clear? It smells a bit . . . odd?' Grant squinted through the crack in the side of his lamp and saw a toilet roll, then right up Billy's nose!

'What's that whispery sound? What's going on with this teapot?' Billy said.

'It's a MAGIC LAMP, thank you **VERY** much!' Grant exclaimed, then quickly clamped his hand over his mouth again.

'Who said that? A magic lamp? Is that a GENIE? Wot? It can't be!' Billy turned the teapot upside down again and shook it hard. 'OW!!!' shouted Grant as more of his possessions fell around him.

'Right, who's in there? If this IS a magic lamp, I guess there's only one way to find out!'

Billy scrunched up some loo roll, spat on it, rubbed the teapot and –

POOOOOF!

– a sparkly cloud of turquoise smoke
appeared and Grant popped out.

'I am Grant, the genie
of this lamp . . .'

'TEAPOT,' fake-
coughed Billy.

'Ahem, I am Grant, the genie of this LAMP and I can grant you THREE wishes.'

'COR, you really **ARE** a genie,' said Billy. 'I thought genies were just from stories in books, not that I read any of those stupid things. Cool! So I can wish for ANYTHING I want, anything at all?'

'Yes,' replied Grant.

Billy leaned back on the toilet. 'WOW –

okay, let me think. First of all I wish for

MORE WISHES!'

'Er, that's against the genie rules, I'm afraid,

but nice try.'

'Uh, stupid rules . . . Okay, genie, first of all

I wish for a lifetime's supply of SWEETS!'

'Coming right up!' said Grant, and he said

his magic wishy word:

'Alaka-blam-a-bumwhistle!'

Suddenly the boys' toilets filled with MEATS – bacon, ham, burgers, sausages. You name it, the room was **FULL** of them.

'GENIE, WHAT HAVE YOU DONE? I said "SWEETS" not "MEATS"! Gross. Urgh, it smells like a pig's bum in here!'

'I do apologise, Billy. I'm still working on my wish-granting, you see, and if I'm nervous, I can sometimes get things even more muddled up. Let me try again.'

'Oh, forget it! The smell has put me off eating anything, even sweets!' Billy said, trying not to be sick. 'I tell you what, though – I want to show Wiggy Wiggins a thing or two for making me his tissue-box holder and embarrassing me in front of the whole school back there. Genie, I wish that the next time the headmaster sneezes he turns into a big fat smelly . . . ELEPHANT! See how he likes THAT!' He cackled.

Grant gulped. He wasn't supposed to do mean wishes, and ever since he'd accidentally turned the genie queen into a snake he'd been super anxious about turning things into animals, but the rules were that he had to grant wishes to whoever rubbed his lamp.

And so . . . Grant closed his eyes, wiggled

his nose and magically appeared in the headmaster's office, keeping small and hidden behind Mr Wiggins who was sitting at his desk drinking a cup of tea and eating a biscuit. Grant couldn't tell if it was a chocolate digestive or a rich tea, but that wasn't important right now.

He whispered, **'Alaka-blam-a-bumwhistle!'**

and the headmaster felt a strange tingly sensation and sat bolt upright in his chair. He felt rather odd, then okay again . . . and carried on eating his biscuit.

Maybe it's a Jammie Dodger, thought Grant, before he wiggled his nose again and reappeared in front of Billy in the boys' loos.

'Oi, where did you go?' Billy asked Grant.

'To grant your wish. All done, I, er, hope. He hasn't sneezed yet, though, so I don't know if it worked, but I'm **SURE** he'll be an elephant in no time, Billy.'

Billy guffawed. 'ha ha, cool! That'll learn him, the pompous old twit! Now for my second wish I want a pet. I don't want your bog-standard boring guinea pig or rabbit; I want something . . . BIG, something scary, the best pet you could possibly have!'

'Oooh, a poodle?'

suggested Grant.

'BORING!' Billy replied.

'What about a cute little piggy?'

'Too fat and smelly.'

'A kitten?' Grant asked, hoping to persuade Billy to wish for something manageable.

Billy's eyes widened.

'Aha, I know! AN

ALLIGATOR!'

Grant frowned and looked nervous.

'Genie, I wish for an ALLIGATOR! And make it snappy!'

'GULP!' gulped Grant, as he closed his eyes, wiggled his nose and said his magic wishy word:

'Alaka-blam-a-bumwhistle!'

And there in front of Grant and Billy was a . . .

'RADIATOR?' Billy moaned. 'I said "ALLIGATOR" not "RADIATOR"!'

'Sorry, Billy,' Grant apologised. 'It's the pressure! I'll try again. **Alaka-blam-a-bUMWhistle!**'

Grant opened his eyes and the radiator was now . . .

'A GLADIATOR?

Well, that's way cooler than a radiator, genie, but still not as cool as a big scary pet. I WANT MY ALLIGATOR NOW!'

The gladiator was just about to ask what was going on when . . .

'Alaka-blam-a-bumWhistle!'

And there finally was . . .

'AN ALLIGATOR, YES!

Thanks, genie. A pet at last, and what a

whopper! I'll call him . . . Arnie!'

The alligator chomped a toilet roll.

And then an actual toilet.

Then the entire toilet cubicle and

belched.

'I'll save my last wish for later, genie – right now I'm going to show off my new pet.'

But before Billy could hop on the alligator it snarled, opened up its jaws and ate through the boys' toilet door and scuttled off into the corridor.

'OH, 'ECK. COME BACK, ARNIE!'

Billy cried.

Grant looked on in HORROR – what had he done?

He needed to find Tilly and Teeny. Where were they?

It was time to put on his detective hat!

CHAPTER 5
LE FRENCH LESSON

Tilly was in a panic – where were Grant and the teapot, and how on earth was she going to find them? Teeny looked at her, raised his nose and sniffed the air.

'Teeny, of course! You can sniff them out!

But how are we going to get out of class?'

They were in French class with Madame Mullet (pronounced Mullaaaaay – the 't' is silent) and everyone was learning the French name for their pets. She went around the class one by one.

'Tia Tricken, you have a . . .'

'A tortoise, Madam Mullet, I mean, Madame Mullaaaaaaay,' replied Tia.

'Ah, *bien*, and the French for tortoise is *LA TORTURE*. All together, everyone . . .'

'*LA TORTURE*,' the class chanted as Madame Mullet waved her arms about like a music conductor.

'EXCELLENT, class. Now, Tilly
Tickleton, you have a . . .'

'A dog, Madame
Mullaaaaaaay, called
Teeny,' Tilly replied.

'Ah yes, and a dog
is *UN CHIEN*. All
together, everyone:

"*UN CHIEN*".

Very good. Now some animals
have exactly the same name
in English **AND** French. For
example, Rachel Ramsbottom,
what is your pet?'

'A rat, madame.'

'YES — a rat! And in French, rat is "*LE rat*"!

Simple, yes? And another example would

be —'

'AN

ALLIGATOR!'

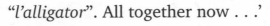

'Er, yes, alligator IS

the same, so we would say

"*l'alligator*". All together now . . .'

But the class just stared behind

Madame Mullet.

'What's wrong? What are you all staring at?'

she questioned.

Tilly pointed behind her.

'L'ALLIGATOR, MADAME!'

Madame Mullet turned round, saw the

enormous scaly monster and screamed.

'AAAAARRRRRRRRGGHHHH!'

All together now: 'AAAAAAAAAAAARGH!'

The whole class screamed and ran as fast as they could away from the big snapping creature.

Birds flapped in panic, hamsters and mice squeaked in TERROR and even Gaby Grant's goldfish was trying to get away from the alligator by swimming round and round in its bowl.

Tilly and Teeny saw their chance and ran out of the door to safety.

'Teeny, get sniffing – we HAVE to find Grant!'

Teeny put his nose to the ground and sniffed away. Having spent the night in a small teapot with him, Teeny certainly had a good idea of what Grant smelled like, so he shouldn't be too hard to find!

CHAPTER 6

CHOCTOPUS!

Grant and Billy saw the alligator run out of the classroom and chased after it, but it was surprisingly speedy. As they turned the corner they could just make out its tail whipping around as it went into the school kitchen.

'We've got to catch it, Grant!'

'How?! It's massive **AND** fast!'

'I dunno! You're the stupid genie – can't you "magic" it somehow?'

Grant was puzzled. 'Why don't you use your third wish?'

'Because I told you before – I want to save it. I'm not wasting it on a stupid alligator – let's hunt for it the normal way.'

Grant **Whizz**ed into his teapot; it was
time to put on one of his special hats
again! Maybe you could
help him choose the
right hat for the
job?

We need a hat that will help

Grant capture the alligator.

What about this one?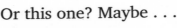

Or this one? Maybe . . .

this one?

Or what about

the one below?

YES, good choice –

this one will be PERFECT!

Grant flew out of the lamp wearing

his animal-watching hat with in-built heat-

scanning binoculars, but was interrupted by

Mr Wiggins making an

announcement over the

school Tannoy system:

BING BONG BING

'I've heard a silly rumour that there is an alligator on the loose in the school grounds. I would like to reassure everyone that this is absolutely absurd. Do **NOT** panic. Clearly some very imaginative troublemakers have been up to mischief, causing poor Madame Mullet to get one of her migraines. All pupils and their pets MUST return to their classes

IMMEDIATELY.'

Grant and Billy sneaked slowly into the kitchen. They couldn't see Arnie anywhere, but they could see a big scary something . . .

Dorothy Mash, the head dinner lady, was in there on her own. The rest of her staff were off with food poisoning, so she was doing all the school dinners herself. She wasn't too happy about this and was muttering what sounded like some rather rude words under her breath.

Billy put his bag with the teapot in it next to the sink and crawled on the floor in search of the alligator, but still couldn't see it.

He carefully crawled around the kitchen, avoiding Mrs Mash, looking in the cupboards,

drawers, fridges and freezers while Grant,

with his heat-scanning binoculars, hovered

around the kitchen. The only things that

showed up in his binoculars were the heat

of all the food being prepared, and Dorothy

Mash, who was very hot and flustered

indeed.

Dorothy put the last big tray of lasagne she was making in the oven and banged the large oven door shut, shouting another rude word. She mopped sweat from her brow with a tea towel.

'Right, just the washing-up to do and I'm out of here,' she humphed.

Dorothy put on a big pair of yellow rubber gloves and started putting all sorts of pots and pans into a huge sink. 'Er, what's this?' She spotted the yellow teapot sticking out of Billy's bag and picked it up.

'As if I haven't got enough to do – people are leaving extra teapots for me to clean!

THIS SCHOOL WILL BE THE END OF ME!'

She grabbed the teapot and started to scrub it with a sponge. 'Honestly, I wish I had more pairs of arms to get all this work done. Ah, and then I'd wish for a nice new hair-do and a big box of my favourite chocolates to relax with!'

Billy and Grant looked at each other.

'Uh-oh, Grant! She just made three wishes in one go while rubbing the teapot!' Billy whispered.

'Tell me something I don't know, Billy,' Grant replied sarcastically before appearing before Mrs Mash.

'I am the genie of this lamp and **YOUR WISHES ARE GRANTED!**' he bellowed.

'EH? A GENIE? LAMP? What's going—' Dorothy shouted.

But before the dinner lady could finish her

sentence, Grant uttered his magic word

'Alaka-blam-a-
bumwhistle!'

and something really odd happened. Dorothy Mash lifted up into the air, turned upside down and started spinning round and round like a Ferris wheel in an apron. 'BLESS ME BUNS, WHAT'S HAPPENING?

she screamed.

AAAAAAAARGH!'

There was a big **POOOOOF** of sparkly turquoise smoke and there, in the middle of the school kitchen, was a large octopus in a dinner-lady uniform with a fancy hair-do eating a big box of chocolates!

'Hmmm, not quite what she'd imagined, Grant,' Billy sniggered.

The octopus blinked at Billy and Grant and carried on doing the dishes while munching the chocolates.

'Er, let's keep looking for the alligator. Come on,' said Grant.

Billy grabbed the teapot and followed him to the schoolyard.

CHAPTER 7

SO CLOSE

No sooner had Grant and Billy gone through one door of the school kitchen, when Teeny burst in through the other, followed by Tilly.

They stopped in their tracks when they saw the chocolate-eating octopus doing the dishes and wearing an apron, with a big fancy hair-do.

'Well, Grant has **DEFINITELY** been here,' Tilly said to Teeny.

Teeny nodded in agreement.

'Sorry to interrupt, Mrs Mash. We'll, er, leave you to it!'

Teeny carried on sniffing out of the door, and they continued searching for Grant, Billy and the teapot, but time was running out. It was nearly time for . . .

*BING

BONG

BING*

'THE PET PARADE WILL
COMMENCE IN THIRTY MINUTES.
I REPEAT, THIRTY MINUTES,'
came the voice of Mr Wiggins over the school
Tannoy again.

'TAKE YOUR PET DIRECTLY TO THE
PLAYING FIELD AND LINE UP IN YOUR
PET CATEGORY: CATS WITH CATS,
RABBITS WITH RABBITS,
ETCETERA, ETCETERA.'

'*Le rats!* We'd better head to the field –
maybe we'll see Billy and Grant on the way,'
said Tilly hopefully. Teeny nodded then put
his nose back to work.

CHAPTER 8

TO THE FIELD!

Grant and Billy had heard the headmaster too. They were now in the school car park where they thought they had just heard Arnie the alligator growling loudly behind the school bus, but it turned out it had been the caretaker, Mr Narksworth, growling loudly as he tried to fix the school bus.

'Mr Wiggins didn't sound much like an elephant to me. Your stupid wish didn't work then, genie,' Billy grunted.

'Sorry, Billy. I thought I might have got that wish right,' replied Grant sadly.

'Well, it seems as though that was just wishful thinking,' Billy said. 'Anyway, don't worry about it now. We'd better head to the playing field for the stupid Pet Parade. We'll have to look for Arnie afterwards.'

And off they ran.

CHAPTER 9

THE PET PARADE

As Tilly and Billy reached the playing field, they could see everyone starting to gather for the Pet Parade. Various pupils were walking around in a large circle with their pets at their sides. On a small stage three teachers

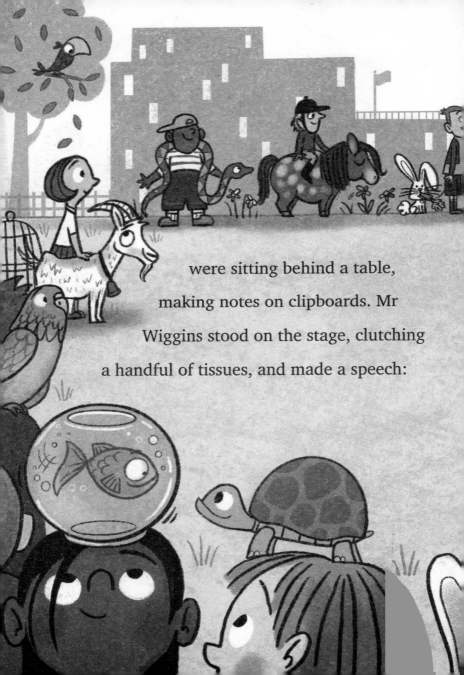

were sitting behind a table,

making notes on clipboards. Mr

Wiggins stood on the stage, clutching

a handful of tissues, and made a speech:

'Boys, girls and pets, welcome to the Pet Parade, where soon we are going to award the

BEST IN SHOW!'

One of the judges stood up and handed a gold envelope to Mr Wiggins.

'I have here a gold envelope and inside is the name of the winning pet . . .'

'MONTY, NO!' someone shouted as their mouse escaped from their grasp. It scampered along the ground, heading straight for the headmaster, then ran right up his trouser leg.

'OOOOOOOH, what's that?' Mr Wiggins shouted. 'There's something tickling my—'

The children started to laugh and point as the headmaster began to wriggle and jiggle like a monkey trying to scratch an itch and eat a banana at the same time.

Suddenly the mouse jumped out from his collar, scuttled up his neck and stood on top of his head. Mr Wiggins looked up and saw the mouse twitching on his toupee.

'Ah . . . ah . . . AH . . . AH . . . AH . . .

ACHOOOOOOOO!'

His sneeze echoed around the field and
his wig shot high into the air, then,

WHOOSH,

there was a huge cloud of turquoise

smoke and then a strange, **LOUD**

TRUMPETY sound.

AH··· AH···

AH··· AH···

ah···

'Ah···

ACHOOOOOOOOO!'

someone in the crowd shouted.

'MR WIGGINS IS A WHOPPING GREAT ELEPHANT!'

Laughs turned to gasps. Nobody could believe their eyes as the wig landed back on the elephant's head with a plop. Tilly knew that voice – it was Billy Krump – and there he was, over by a tree with Grant sitting on his shoulder!

Grant beamed. 'YES! Billy, it **WORKED.** I AM getting better at this wish malarkey!'

'Nice one, genie,' said Billy, and the pair high-fived.

Tilly ran over. 'GRANT! Are you okay? What's Billy been doing to you?' she asked sternly.

'Don't worry, Tilly – he's not so bad. Well, apart from smelling like meat and wishing Mr Wiggins was an elephant!' Grant giggled.

'Oh, that was **YOUR** idea, was it, Billy? That was actually quite funny, but we'd better turn him back.'

'Spoilsport.'

But before Grant could even TRY to turn him back to normal, the stage started to wobble and crack under the elephant's weight. The judges all dived off and rolled on to the grass just before it crashed to the ground. But the sound scared all the animals and they started to SQUAWK, **BARK** and SCREECH. Some of the animals freed themselves from

their leads or cages and started to run around the playing field, their owners chasing after them. It was CHAOS!

The mouse (who was still on Mr Wiggins's wig) made a run for it and slid down his long grey trunk and escaped just before . . .

'A-A-A-AH-AH-AH- ACHOOOOOOOOO!'

There was another large

WHOOSH,

and a cloud of turquoise smoke

appeared again.

Mr Wiggins wasn't an

elephant any more.

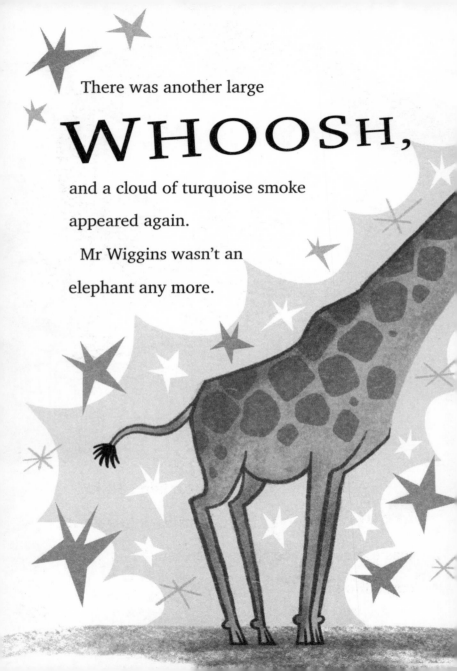

'He's a . . . a GIRAFFE!' exclaimed Billy.

'WHOOPS,' gulped Grant. 'I thought it was too good to be true. When will I ever get something right?'

The Mr Wiggins giraffe looked as confused as everyone else as it lolloped awkwardly around the field on its long wonky legs. The wig slipped over its eyes so it couldn't see that it was nearly treading on animals and children! The teachers didn't know what to do, so they just started blowing their whistles and shouting for calm. There were pets and children running around EVERYWHERE!

'A-A-A-A-A-A-AH-AH-AH-ACHOOOOOOOO!'

'Not again?' said Tilly.

This time Mr Wiggins transformed into a

HIPPOPOTAMUS!

'ACHOOOOOOO!'

Then a

GORILLA!

'GRANT, WHAT'S GOING ON?'

Tilly shouted over all the screaming.

'I don't know. I guess my wish powers are stronger than I thought!' he shouted back.

'We need to do something or someone's going to get hurt!'

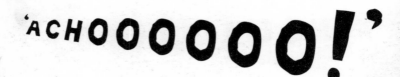

'ACHOOOOOOO!'

Now Mr Wiggins

was a

T. REX!

'What next?' shouted Tilly. 'He's getting bigger and **bigger!** Now he's a

WHALE!'

OOOOO!

'Oh, hang on, now he's . . . disappeared!'

'Where is he? Where's he gone?' they asked
each other.

'THERE HE IS, TILLY!'

Billy shouted. 'HE'S A CHICKEN!
A chicken with a wig on! Ha ha!'
The sight of the Mr Wiggins chicken

running around with a wig

on WAS very funny. But

what happened

next was **NOT**.

Because from round the side of the school building came a very hungry, very snappy-looking Arnie the alligator. He started chasing anything that looked like food, which was basically everything on the playing field!

'BERGEEEERK!'

squawked Mr Wiggins, flapping into the air.

This got Arnie's attention and stealthily he started crawling towards Mr Wiggins. He was getting closer and closer, opening his jaws as wide as he could, ready to munch the poor chicken when Billy shouted:

'GENIE, for my third wish I want **EVERYTHING** to go back to normal!'

'Phew, I thought you'd never ask,' replied Grant.

He flew up into the air, closed his eyes, wiggled his nose and shouted,

'Alaka-blam-a-bumwhistle!'

There was a final huge WHOOSH,
and the biggest cloud of turquoise smoke yet,
then everything went back to normal . . .

Tilly, Teeny, Billy and Grant were back in a
large circle of pupils and pets who were all calm.

Everyone's pets were back on their leads or in their cages or bowls, and everyone was waiting to hear who had the winning pet.

Tilly breathed a sigh of relief. 'I don't think anyone remembers what happened all day! Nice one, Grant – that could have been **VERY** tricky to explain to Mum when we get home!'

'I have here a gold envelope and inside is the name of the winning pet . . .' started Mr Wiggins, who was ACTUALLY Mr Wiggins again.

Grant sat on Tilly's shoulder.

'Wow, well done, Grant. You did it – you got a wish right. I knew you could do it,' she said, beaming.

Teeny gave him a lovely big lick and Grant hugged him back.

'The winner is Polly Parker's pet poodle, Petunia!' announced Mr Wiggins, clapping.

Grant sighed. 'Aw, I do love a poodle.' Teeny looked a bit offended. 'Don't worry, Teeny, you're still **OUR** winner!'

'Congratulations, Polly and Petunia, and thank you all for a very eventful Bring Your Pet to School Day. And because I am in such a good mood, and as you have all done so well today, you are free to go home early!'

The crowd of pupils cheered:
'**HOORAY!**' They were all relieved
that they wouldn't have to eat Mrs Mash's
disgusting school dinners.

'Now have a safe journey home and I will
see you all bright and early at the start of
next term.'

Mr Wiggins turned round to walk off
the stage and the entire school burst
out laughing.

There, sticking out of the back of the headmaster's trousers, was an elephant's tail swishing left and right!

"WHOOPS!" said Grant.

He quickly clicked his fingers and it vanished.

CHAPTER 10

A TEENY OFFER

Tilly packed up her rucksack and started to walk home with Grant perched on her shoulder again.

'Well, that was an eventful day, guys!' she said, exhausted. 'Not sure if I could take you both to school EVERY day, but it certainly was quite an adventure. It's a shame in a way that nobody else can remember it, especially Billy. He came good in the end, didn't he?'

Grant nodded. 'Hey, he's over there. Why don't you go over and talk to him?' he suggested.

'That's a nice idea, Grant. Might be worth a try.' Tilly walked up to Billy.

'What you want, Tilly-Tutu?'

'I was wondering, Billy, seeing as you don't have a pet and all . . . if you might want to play with Teeny and me sometimes. You could even walk him the odd time too, if you wanted to, that is?'

Billy was puzzled. 'Eh, what you after?'

'Nothing. I just thought it might be fun,'
Tilly said, smiling.

'Er, yeah, that would be all right, er, thanks?'

Teeny jumped into his arms and licked the
side of his face.

'Hee hee, get off, you,' he giggled, and put Teeny back on the ground. 'Well, this is me,' he said, pointing at his house. 'I'll see you next week at school.'

Billy walked up his driveway with a hopeful smile on his face and turned back and waved at Tilly and Teeny – and was that a blue thing waving back on Tilly's shoulder? Nah, he must be seeing things, he thought to himself, and carried on into his house.

CHAPTER 11
BACK HOME

'Right, Grant, when we get home, I want you to go back into your lamp for a bit and wait until I'm in my bedroom, okay? Once I've finished chatting with Mum we can talk more about Genie World and what me and Teeny can do to help you get home.'

'Thanks, Tilly.' And Grant magicked himself back into his lamp where he made himself a nice cup of snot chocolate, which **SHOULD** of course have been hot chocolate.

'HI, MUM. WE'RE HOME!'

'Hello, darling. You're home early.'

'Yeah, Mr Wiggins let us off as it's the end of term,' Tilly replied.

'Do you want me to get you some lunch?'

Teeny nodded and looked at his empty bowl.

'Yes, please,' said Tilly. 'We're starving!'

'Did you and Teeny have a good day at school?'

'It was fine. Same old, same old. But we

didn't win best in show at the **Pet Parade**.'

'Oh, never mind, love – winning isn't everything. Here you go.' And Tilly's mum put down a plate of sausages, mash and gravy for Tilly, and a bowl of sausages for Teeny.

Grant got a whiff of the
sausages and held his nose;
he'd had enough of the
smell of meat today!
Tilly and Teeny wolfed down
their food at super-quick speed.

'Hey, slow down, you two! You'll get
indigestion!'

Teeny burped.

'Sorry, Mum, lots of homework to do!'

'ACHOOOOOO!'

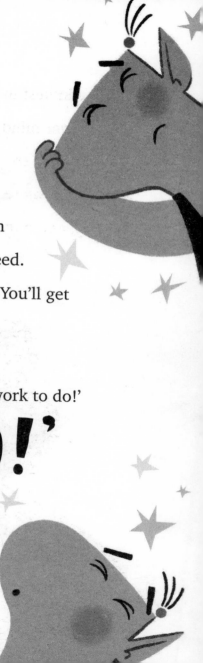

A sneeze came
from the
teapot lamp.

'What was that, Tilly?'

Tilly pretended to sneeze.

'ACHOOOOOOO!

It's just all the fluff up my nose from all the pets at school, Mum. Right, I'd better get on with my homework.'

She excused herself from the table and ran
upstairs to her bedroom and closed the door.

She placed the teapot on the bed and Teeny
jumped up beside them.

'Grant, are you okay? You can come out now!'

Tilly was nervous about how Grant might look. Would the sneezing wish really be gone? Or would it work on him? Would he be an elephant, a T. rex, a goodness-knows-what?

There was a little puff of smoke and there was Grant, right as rain, looking perfectly normal, except he was wearing an apron and holding a feather duster.

'Yes, I'm fine! I was just tidying up my lamp after Billy shook it so much earlier and the dust got up my nose.'

Tilly giggled. 'Phew. Now, can you tell me more about Genie World . . . ?'

Grant sat down and started to explain everything that had happened back in Genie World before he had arrived on Earth, from turning the genie queen into a snake after she had mistakenly thought he was a chef, to him getting banished, right down to his lamp being thrown down to Earth by the royal genie guards.

'What about your family, Grant? They must be missing you terribly.'

'I really miss my dad and little sister, but they might not have noticed I've gone yet. They're a little, er, unusual like me,' Grant said.

Tilly was puzzled. 'How do you mean?'

'Well, my dad's a "genie of all trades" – he's really creative, has a heart of gold and loves to help everyone. The problem is that he's rather clumsy, and some of the jobs he does can go a bit . . . wrong . . . Like the time he was giving one of our neighbours flying-carpet lessons and decided to show them how to do a loop-the-loop.'

'What went wrong?' Tilly asked.

'Well, I won't go into details, but the loop-the-loop ended up being more poop-the-poop!' Grant chuckled. 'And even though my little sister is super annoying, she's also hilarious. A couple of years ago we were playing hide-and-seek and she magicked herself invisible but couldn't undo the spell and we couldn't find her for six months!'

Tilly giggled. 'I'm sure your family will have noticed you're gone and are doing all they can to find you. You'll be back with them one day soon, and maybe I could meet them too! Teeny and I will do everything we can to help, won't we, boy?'

Teeny woofed and licked Grant, which cheered him up.

'Thank you. I do love Earth, though, Tilly. It's been **SO** much fun and there's still so much for me to explore! Let me get my book and I'll show you what else I'd like to see. Actually, Tilly, Teeny, I tell you what . . . do you want to come INTO the lamp and I can show you everything?'

'Oh yes, please, Grant! I'd love to!' Tilly grinned and Teeny woofed excitedly.

'Okay, now I'll calmly try to get this right first time . . .'

He closed his eyes and focused on Tilly and Teeny, wiggled his nose and clicked his fingers.

CRASH!

THE TEAPOT
GREW
SO LARGE

'Tilly, what's going on up there?' her mum shouted up the stairs.

'IT'S okay, MUM. JUST, ER . . .

A SCIENCE EXPERIMENT!'

'WHOOPS, sorry again!'

Grant closed his eyes, tighter this time, wiggled his nose and clicked his fingers again.

This time the teapot SHRANK and spun faster and FASTER until it was teapot size again and landed back on Tilly's bed. Then Tilly and

Teeny SHRANK too, and
the lid lifted off the
teapot and they flew
inside!

145

'WOW, Grant, that was AMAZING!
And just look at this place!'

Tilly was in awe.

She walked
around, gazing at
all the hats, potions,

books and other amazing objects inside the
lamp. She couldn't believe that she was
actually in a **REAL** magical lamp!
There was even a
toilet!

And a little kitchen!
She loved EVERYTHING
about it.

She jumped on to Grant's bed and started
asking him lots of questions. 'So how does
magic work? Why do people only get three
wishes? Ooooh, when can I get **MY** three
wishes? Has Teeny had three wishes? Can
you speak Dog? Can you teach me magic?'

'Whoa, slow down, Tilly! I've got SO much

to show you, but I think you should have a nap first; it's been a **VERY** long day!'

'I'm not tired. I could stay awake aaaall night!' she said, pretending not to yawn, even though she was really tired and was, in fact, trying really hard to stay awake.

'Let me read you some jokes from my favourite book!'

Grant got **THE BIGGEST GENIE JOKE BOOK EVER** down from the shelf and opened it at a random page.

'So, Tilly, **what do you call an
alligator in a vest** ...

An InVESTigator!

HA HA HA HA!'

Tilly giggled, still trying not to yawn.

'And, Teeny, **what do you call a bee
with a magic spell on him?**

BEE-WITCHED!

HA HA HA HA HA!'

Teeny groaned and snuggled up next to Tilly on Grant's bed.

'Okay, here's a great one, guys: **why did the octopus blush?**

Because it saw the ocean's bottom!

HA HA **HA HA HA!**

That's the best one today. What do you think?'

Grant laughed his head off and wondered why Tilly wasn't laughing her head off too. He turned to look at her and saw that she was fast asleep with Teeny snoring next to her.

Grant stretched and yawned, put on his sleeping cap and got into his hammock. What a day they'd had, an exhausting but magically wonderful and funny day. Grant looked up at a picture of him and his family on a shelf. He felt a bit sad, but knew he would see them again one day.

He lay down and fell straight to sleep.

Have a nice nap, Genie, Teeny and Tilly.

EXTRA UNEXPECTED CHAPTER

MUM'S DISCOVERY

'You okay in here, you two?' asked Tilly's mum as she opened her bedroom door, holding out a mug of hot chocolate. 'Where are you? Tilly? Teeny?'

She looked under the bed, in the wardrobe and behind the curtains. 'Are you hiding from me again? Come on, Tilly! This isn't funny.'

Then she heard a strange faint snoring that sounded as if it was coming from the yellow teapot on the bed . . .

TO BE CONTINUED . . .

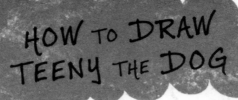

HOW TO DRAW TEENY THE DOG

Start with a triangle and draw three dots either side.

Add ovals for eyes and a smiley mouth.

Draw two circles for his pupils and two lines for his eyebrows.

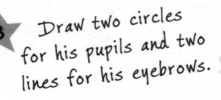

 Draw the curly fur around his face.

 Then add his curly ears and fluffy eyebrow detail.

 Next, add his collar and a circle for his dog tag. Put the letter 'T' inside it.

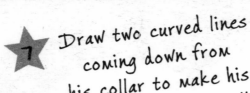

Draw two curved lines coming down from his collar to make his front legs. Add small lines for his toes.

8

Add his two hind legs and toe lines.

9

Finally add his waggy tail, then colour him in!

DRAW YOUR TEENY HERE!

STEVEN LENTON is a multi-award-winning illustrator, originally from Cheshire, now working from his studios in Brighton and London with his French bulldog, Big-Eared Bob!

He has illustrated many children's books, including *Head Kid* and *Future Friend* by David Baddiel, *The Hundred and One Dalmatians* adapted by Peter Bently, the Shifty McGifty and Slippery Sam series by Tracey Corderoy, Frank Cottrell-Boyce's fiction titles and Steven Butler's Sainsbury's Prize-winning The Nothing to See Here Hotel series.

He has illustrated two World Book Day titles and regularly appears at literary festivals, live events and schools across the UK.

Steven has his own Draw-Along-A-Lenton YouTube channel, showing you how to draw a range of his characters, and he was in the Top 20 Bookseller Bestselling Illustrator Chart 2019.

The Genie and Teeny series is Steven's first foray into children's fiction and he really hopes you are enjoying Grant and Teeny's adventures!

Find out more about Steven and his work at stevenlenton.com.